The Pen That Pa Built

by **DAVID EDWARDS** • Illustrations by **ASHLEY WOLFF**

TRICYCLE PRESS
Berkeley/Toronto

who live in the pen that Pa built.

who live in the
pen that Pa built.

who live in the pen that Pa built.

A WORD ABOUT WOOL

Now you know how a rural family in the mid-19th century made a blanket. But did you know the process continues today?

Sheep are sheared once a year, in spring or early summer. Most sheep shearers today use power shears. With practice, a person can shear more than two hundred sheep a day!

The wool is washed to remove dirt and oils before being carded. Carding wool means passing it through wire teeth. Like a series of combs, these teeth remove tangles. The result is a flat sheet of wool. This sheet of wool is called a web, because it looks like a spider's web.

The web of wool is rolled into narrow strands called slivers. The slivers are stretched and twisted into yarn on a loom or spinning machine.

Most natural dyes come from parts of plants—berries, bark, leaves, flowers, and roots.

The yellow dye in this story came from goldenrod. In order to get the best color—the brightest yellow—it's important to cut the flowers when they are in full bloom, but watch out for bees!

Indigo, a dark blue dye, comes from the leaves of the woad plant. It was used to color the blue coats of Colonial soldiers during the American Revolution.

The madder plant, a prickly vine, makes a bright red dye. It was used to color the jackets worn by British soldiers during the American Revolution—that's why they were nicknamed the redcoats.

The dyed yarn may be knitted into sweaters, scarves, mittens, and socks or wove on a loom into blankets or cloth. Wool cloth can be cut and sewn into coats, pants, and other warm clothes.

And what happens to the sheep?

The sheep will grow more wool to keep them warm in winter. Then the shearing and carding and spinning and weaving all begin again next spring.

For Adele, the answer to my prayers, and to David, Steven, Deirdre and Christianna, our blessings—D.E.

For all the brave and capable fathers I admire, especially Klaus and Bud, Sabin, Courtenay and Chad—A.W.

Text copyright © 2007 by David Edwards
Illustrations copyright © 2007 by Ashley Wolff

TRICYCLE PRESS
an imprint of Ten Speed Press
PO Box 7123
Berkeley, California 94707
www.tricyclepress.com

Design by Susan Van Horn
Typeset in Old Claude, Horley Old Style, and Windsor Antique
The illustrations in this book were created with black gesso and gouache on Arches Cover.

Library of Congress Cataloging-in-Publication Data

Edwards, David, 1962 Dec. 29-
The pen that Pa built / by David Edwards ; illustrations by Ashley Wolff.
p. cm.
Summary: A cumulative, illustrated tale describing the process of raising
sheep and using their wool to make warm woolen blankets.
ISBN-13: 978-1-58246-153-3
ISBN-10: 1-58246-153-8
[1. Sheep—Fiction. 2. Sheep ranches—Fiction.] I. Wolff, Ashley, ill. II. Title.
PZ8.3.E263Pen 2007
[E]—dc22
2006101994
First Tricycle Press printing, 2007
Printed in China

1 2 3 4 5 6 — 12 11 10 09 08 07